ANGRY

A SIDE-SPLITTING, RIB-TICKLING JOKE BOOK

CHEEP LAUGHS

EGMONT

We bring stories to life

First published in Great Britain 2012 by Egmont UK Limited
The Yellow Building, 1 Nicholas Road, London W11 4AN

ISBN 978 1 4052 6657 4
54817/1
Printed in Great Britain

WHAT GOES GREY, YELLOW, GREY, YELLOW, GREY, YELLOW?

An elephant rolling down the hill with a daffodil in its mouth.

WHAT'S A CROCODILE'S FAVOURITE CARD GAME?

Snap!

WHAT DOES A CAT EAT FOR BREAKFAST?

Mice Crispies.

WHERE DO YOU FIND GIANT SNAILS?

At the end of the giant's fingers!

WHAT DO YOU CALL TWO THIEVES?

A pair of nickers!

WHAT FISH ONLY SWIMS AT NIGHT?

A starfish!

RIB TICKLERS

WHAT'S THE WORST THING ABOUT BEING AN OCTOPUS?
Washing your hands before dinner.

HOW CAN YOU TELL IF AN ELEPHANT HAS BEEN IN YOUR REFRIGERATOR?
There are footprints in the butter.

WHY DID THE BANANA GO TO THE DOCTOR?
Because it wasn't peeling well!

WHY SHOULDN'T YOU TELL AN EGG A JOKE?
Because it might crack up!

HOW DO YOU STOP YOUR NOSE FROM RUNNING?
Teach it to hop!

WHAT DO YOU CALL A CRAFTY PIG?
Cunningham!

WHICH FISH IS THE SLEEPIEST?
A kipper.

WHY DID THE SCARECROW WIN AN AWARD?
Because he was out-standing in his field!

WHY IS A TRACTOR MAGIC?
Because it can go down a road and turn into a field!

HOW DOES
A PIG SIGN A
LETTER?
With hogs and
kisses.

WHAT'S THE
BEST DAY FOR
A PIG TO EAT
SOMETHING
TOUGH?
(Chews-day!)

WHY DO PIGS LIKE JOKES ABOUT FOOD?
Because they're always in good taste.

PIGS ARE SO STUPID,
THEY TRY TO THROW
BIRDS OFF A CLIFF ...

WHY ARE PIGS ALWAYS FULL?
Because they pig out
at every meal!

PORKERS

WHAT'S A PIG'S FAVOURITE PLAY?
Hamlet!

WHAT DO YOU CALL A PIG WITH LOADS OF CASH?
Filthy rich!

WHY DOES A PIG LOVE HISTORY?
Because it's full of dates!

WHAT'S A PIG'S FAVOURITE SCARY MOVIE?
Frankenswine!

WHY DON'T PIGS LIKE NUTS?
It's chest-nut their type of food!

ANGRY BIRDS

A SIDE-SPLITTING, RIB-TICKLING JOKE BOOK

SNOUTRAGEOUS!

EGMONT

We bring stories to life

First published in Great Britain 2012 by Egmont UK Limited
The Yellow Building, 1 Nicholas Road, London W11 4AN

ISBN 978 1 4052 6657 4
54817/1
Printed in Great Britain